AI

4195

£1

CW00727845

THE
ORPHAN
AND THE
BILLIONAIRE

Also by Patrick Skene Catling

THE CHOCOLATE TOUCH

PATRICK SKENE CATLING

THE
ORPHAN
AND THE
BILLIONAIRE

Methuen

For
Sasha & Sophia
and
Alexander & Alistair

First published in Great Britain 1990
by Methuen Children's Books
Michelin House, 81 Fulham Road, London, SW3 6RB
Copyright © 1990 Patrick Skene Catling
Printed in Great Britain by St Edmundsbury Press,
Bury St Edmunds, Suffolk

British Library Cataloguing in Publication Data

Catling, Patrick Skene
The orphan and the billionaire.
I. Title
823'.912 [J]

ISBN 0–416–15472–7

Contents

One

An Unfortunate Accident

As soon as Michael got home on the fine spring afternoon that changed his life, he went to the kitchen, as usual, to get a glass of milk and check up on the cakes.

He had just opened the fridge when he heard the busy *squeak squeak* of Mrs Fox's rubber-soled shoes approaching along the hall. Mrs Fox was the housekeeper. She had looked after the house and Michael ever since his mother had died when he was a baby. Of course, he could not remember his mother, but his father had often shown him some beautiful photographs of her.

Michael certainly knew that Mrs Fox was different. She was nothing like any of his friends' mothers. She was a small, fussy woman, with frizzy hair dyed orange, thick glasses, a sharp, mauve nose and thin lips, who smelled of sickly-sweet deodorant. She was the sort of woman who would hurt the inside of your ear if she poked a washcloth into it. She always smiled a lot when Michael's father was at home but hardly ever when he was out.

'Oh, you're back, Michael!' she exclaimed now, as if he did not already know that. 'Sit down,' she ordered him in her hard, nasal voice. (If you want to know what it sounded like, try pinching the end of your nose while you speak.) 'I'm afraid I have some bad news for you.'

She did not look afraid. She looked strangely eager.

Michael sat down beside the table and wondered what was wrong. Had he done something she thought he shouldn't have done?

'It's Mr Chapman,' she said. On serious occasions, she called Michael's father 'Mr Chapman'. 'Mr Chapman isn't going to like that,' she would warn Michael. 'Wait till I tell Mr Chapman.' When she did, Michael's father always forgave him. Michael was his father's only child. They were very good friends. But Mrs Fox's complaints, as she meant them to be, could be embarrassing. This time something about her manner made her sound extra-serious.

'Mr Chapman has had an accident,' she said. 'Unfortunately, it was his fault. He drove through a red light and hit a bus. They took him to hospital.'

Michael felt the first prickle of alarm. His heart thumped.

'How is he? When can I go to see him?'

'He was a real mess,' she said coldly. 'There was nothing the doctor could do. Your daddy has passed away.'

'You mean. . . ?' Michael began, but he could not say any more.

'That's right. I mean he's dead. And it's no use

8

crying. That won't bring him back to life.' She stared at him for a moment. Her little brown eyes were shining. 'There are going to be some changes here. Big changes.'

Two

Trouble With Cuddles

When Michael's father had been alive, the Foxes had lived in their own flat, in the basement.

Charlie Fox was an awful slob. He was bald and fat and sweaty and he did not often change his underwear and socks. On weekdays, with much grumbling, he went to work as an assistant cook in a neighbouring pizzeria. On Saturdays and Sundays he got out of bed late and never shaved, so by the end of the weekend his fat face became rough with grey stubble. He sniffed and snorted and spat a lot, like a pig with hay fever. Until noon his watery blue eyes were pink around the edges. He lolled about in a dingy PIZZA HEAVEN T-shirt that bulged over the belt of his jeans, watched television, drank beer out of the bottles, smoked horrible little cigars and nagged his wife. Not surprisingly, she had not kissed him for several years, and he was in a permanently bad mood. 'You behave as if the world is your ashtray,' she used to say. What he said back is too unpleasant to be repeated.

The Foxes had a daughter, a year or two younger

than Michael. Her name was Shirlene but her parents called her Cuddles. She had dark yellow hair, blue eyes and skin as white as raw dough. Perhaps because she ate so much pizza and pies covered with whipped cream, she was already quite pudgy. She had dimples in her cheeks, elbows, knees and some other places. Even her dimples had dimples. Mr and Mrs Fox thought Cuddles' dimples were adorable and often said so.

'I wish the Foxes would go away,' Michael had said to his father.

But Mr Fox had seen them only when they were pretending to be nice.

'They've been with us for years. We mustn't be unkind. Poor Charlie works hard and he has a chest problem.'

So the Foxes had stayed. Now Michael was an orphan, with absolutely no relations he could call on for help. He knew he was at the Foxes' mercy.

After the funeral, which was simple and quick, the first change took place. The Foxes took over the upper part of the house while Michael was at school. When he came home he was about to go up to his room to do his homework when Mrs Fox stopped him.

'Michael! From now on, you're in the basement.'

'But that's where you live, Mrs Fox!' he protested. Sharing rooms with them would be really disgusting.

'Not any more,' she said, smiling. 'It will be more convenient if we change places. We'll have more space upstairs and so will you downstairs. It's the logical thing to do.'

'But, Mrs Fox, I want to stay in my own room. It's always been my room. Please, Mrs Fox. All my things are there.'

'You collected a lot of junk that you'll be better off without. I've already started getting the room ready for Cuddles. Let's not have any silly arguments. You've got to learn that what I say around here goes.'

Mrs Fox now had the main bedroom, Mr Fox had the guest room and Cuddles had Michael's room. There was nothing he could do about it.

He went up to what had been his room and found the fat girl sitting at his desk, drawing with his coloured pencils in his drawing book.

'Hey! Those are mine!'

'Who says?' Cuddles asked with a teasing grin.

'You know they are.'

'I asked Mum if I could use them and she said I could. If you try to take them I'll scream and you'll be in trouble.'

'What's happened to my posters?' he demanded, looking around the room. There were pale, blank spaces on the walls where he had taped his posters to 'SAVE THE DOLPHINS' and 'PLANT A TREE' and a big photograph of the first men on the moon. 'And where's my model of the Mayflower?'

'Gone,' Cuddles said casually. 'I suppose Mum dumped them in the incinerator.'

'In the *incinerator!*'

'That's what I said. It's where we put boring old posters and other rubbish.'

'It took me weeks to make that ship,' he said.

'You wasted a lot of time then, didn't you?'

12

'It was an authentic scale model. Every bit of rigging, every sail –'

'Mum said it was a dust trap. It could have given me an allergy. Anyway, I didn't like it. It was so old-fashioned.'

He went over to the bed and looked under the quilt. Cuddles again grinned nastily.

'Rubbish,' she said.

She knew he was searching for his teddy bear, which had been his companion as long as he could remember. Its brown fur was patchy and faded with age. Once a dog had attacked it, badly tearing an arm, and it had had to have an operation in a dolls' hospital. He knew he was rather old for a teddy bear but he loved it.

'You didn't . . .' he began.

'We did, if you're wondering about that ratty old bear. Mum said it must have been full of germs, and it was time you grew up. I don't have dolls any more, and you're a boy. Now, get out of my room. Mum said if you annoy me you'll be sorry.'

Mrs Fox gave Michael a slice of cold pizza for supper that evening in the small kitchen in the basement. It was the worst pizza he had ever had, a stale leftover, rubbery cheese on soggy pastry. Sitting alone, he could hear music and loud laughter in the kitchen above.

The basement bed-linen had not been changed. One bed smelled of carnation deodorant. Another smelled of cigars and sweat. He settled reluctantly in the third bed, although it smelled of Cuddles.

Missing his father and thinking about the meanness of the Foxes, he did something he had not

13

done since the day of the funeral. He wept and wept and wept. By morning his pillow was damp with tears, and he was determined to make changes of his own.

Three

Ready, Steady, Go!

Michael dressed in his usual school clothes, but after eating his breakfast cornflakes he repacked his satchel. He took out all his school things and put in some of the favourite books his father had read to him and that Michael sometimes read again himself – *Alice's Adventures in Wonderland* by Lewis Carroll; *Zelda's Ogre* by Tomi Ungerer, and *Charlotte's Web* by E. B. White. He added his atlas, because he enjoyed looking at maps and imagining all the lands and seas of the world. These were the few books he'd had time to grab from his bedroom. He packed underwear, socks, a T-shirt, a small towel, soap, toothpaste and his toothbrush and a comb.

The bag was bulging. Had he forgotten anything important? Food! He made a jam sandwich and stuck that in. He had very little money, only a few pounds he had earned mowing lawns and washing cars.

Then he went to the garage for his bicycle, his most valuable possession, a shiny red and silver one with gears – his father's last birthday present to him. It was in its proper place, leaning against the wall beside his father's car. But the bicycle's back wheel was secured by a new chain and padlock.

Mrs Fox was in 'her' kitchen, cooking bacon and eggs.

'There's a lock on my bike, Mrs Fox,' he said.

'That's so nobody can steal it,' she said, with a challenging glint in her eyes.

'Well, please may I have the key? I've got to go now.'

'No, you may not. Mr Fox is taking the bicycle back to the shop.'

'You're not selling my bike!'

'It costs money to feed you,' she pointed out.

'Didn't my father leave enough for that? His house and everything –'

'Now, now, nosey,' she interrupted him. The Foxes often interrupted. 'Small boys shouldn't poke their noses into legal matters they can't understand. We're attending to all that sort of business about money and so on. You just run along to school. Can't you see I'm busy making our breakfast?'

'I have a long way to go,' he said, quite truthfully. His school was nearly two miles away and he planned to go a lot farther than that.

'You'd better get a move on, then, or you'll be late.'

'I suppose Mr Fox is going to take Cuddles in the car,' Michael said bitterly. They were so unfair about everything.

'That's no concern of yours. But, as a matter of fact, as it happens, he is going to drive her. I think

16

she may have the beginnings of a cold. The little dear gets overtired.'

At that moment, the little dear took her place at the table, eagerly licking her fat lips.

Michael turned and left, lugging his heavy satchel.

Four

Good Weather for Pie

First he walked to the bus station.

'What's the fare to Wales?' he asked the man at the ticket-window. 'Or Scotland?' Michael knew they were both far away.

'Where exactly are you meant to be going? There's a difference.'

'Where are the best cattle?' Michael wanted to know. He had sometimes thought he would quite like to be a cowboy, if he could learn to ride a horse.

'What's this, some sort of game you're playing?' the ticket-seller demanded, frowning impatiently.

'Come on, sonny,' said a man in the queue that was lengthening behind Michael. 'Make up your mind. I have a bus to catch.'

The ticket-seller told Michael the fare to Bristol.

'Oh,' Michael said. He had not known that bus tickets were so expensive. 'I'll come back another time. Thanks anyway.'

As he turned away, the man behind him shook his head and commented: 'The young of today! Where do they get their crazy ideas?'

Michael did not want to explain his difficulties to strangers, so he kept going.

Outside the station, he decided that he would travel in a westerly direction, the opposite way to school. He would have to try to hitch a lift. His father had advised him against hitch-hiking, because you never knew what sort of person might pick you up. In the present, exceptional circumstances, however, Michael felt that his father would have understood the need to take risks.

Walking by factories and filling stations and open spaces littered with rubbish, Michael went along the left verge of a motorway, waving his upraised right thumb, but no drivers stopped or even slowed down. A short distance beyond the edge of the town, however, at a crossroads, he stood beside a stop sign with his thumb held high. Drivers had to pause there for a moment, whether they wanted to or not, so he thought he would have a fair chance of a ride.

Sure enough, after a few minutes, a great diesel juggernaut wheezed to a halt, its cabin door swung open, and a friendly-looking driver in green overalls shouted down to him: 'Jump in, lad!' Michael clambered up the steep metal steps and sat on the wide, plastic-covered seat, the driver leaned over and slammed the door, and they were on their way.

He turned down the volume of the country and western music on the stereo, so that they could hear each other speak.

'My name's Josh Driscoll,' he said, strongly shaking Michael's hand. 'What's yours?'

'Michael Chapman.'

'OK, Mike. Welcome aboard. I've been on the road all night. You can help me stay awake.'

Michael glanced a little anxiously at Josh's eyes. They seemed to be open wide enough. He looked at the speedometer: 75 miles an hour. Josh noticed where Michael was looking and seemed to read his mind.

'I wish this thing would go faster,' the driver said with a grin. 'The sooner I get home, the happier I'll be.' Home, Michael thought. Now he had no home.

They drove along steadily without talking, while a woman sang sadly about love, and Josh kept time with his fingers dancing on the steering wheel. Then he said:

'Have you come far, Mike?'

'Not very far,' Michael replied, trying to sound as if he had come quite far. More candidly, he added: 'This is my first lift. I was walking.'

'No school today?'

Michael squirmed and blushed.

'No school for you at least, right?' Josh said, chuckling sympathetically. 'It's nice, having your own, special, personal, private, exclusive holiday, isn't it?'

'I'm heading out west,' Michael said, in a television cowboy voice.

'No foolin', pardner?' Josh said. 'What are you goin' to do out yonder? You sure is travellin' light.'

'I don't know yet,' Michael admitted. Anything I can. I'll have to find a job.'

The driver twisted his nose from side to side and back again, a face people sometimes make when they are doubtful.

'That sounds very ambitious,' he said politely. 'The best of luck to you.'

The first big raindrops of a heavy shower suddenly started splashing against the windscreen. Josh switched on the wipers, which could hardly keep the glass clear. Low, dark grey clouds were obscuring the blue sky. Michael had not thought of wearing his raincoat.

'Not very good weather for hitch-hiking. Anyway, here we are. Home, sweet home. And in time for lunch. You can wait here till the rain stops,' Josh said.

He braked and turned off the motorway into a car-park beside a one-storey building with a neon sign that said: CAFÉ.

'I'd better go on, thanks,' Michael said, thinking about money. 'And thanks for the ride.'

'Oh, come on! You'd be daft to stand out in this. You'd get soaked. Don't you like lemon meringue pie?'

'Thanks, but I'm not hungry,' Michael said, which was not true. 'I had a late breakfast. But maybe I'd better come in for a while.'

They ran into the café, which was a cheerful place, bright and warm. They sat on red-topped stools at a red counter. A pretty, young woman behind the counter smiled and handed over menus, then surprised Michael by giving Josh a big kiss.

'This is Anna,' he said, wiping the red smudge off his cheek with the back of his hand. 'She doesn't kiss *all* the customers. My wife. Anna, this is Mike. He's heading out west, but now it's raining, so he's

21

stopping with us for a bite to eat.'

'Aren't you a bit young to be travelling alone?' Anna asked.

'Well . . .' Michael said.

'It depends, doesn't it, Mike?' Josh suggested helpfully.

'Yes. It depends.'

'Let's talk about food,' Josh said. 'What's today's special?'

'Steak and kidney pie,' Anna said encouragingly. 'There's plenty of good, thick gravy. Mixed veg.'

Michael's mouth watered inside. He gulped.

'Thanks, but I brought a sandwich. If I could just have a glass of milk . . .' He blushed. 'I'm on a budget.'

'Who isn't, mate?' Josh said, patting Michael on the shoulder. 'We know all about budgets, don't we, Anna? We're saving to buy a house. We live in a small caravan round the back here.'

'Two steak and kidney pies then!' Anna said.

She went back through swinging doors and told the cook.

Michael thought they were the kindest people he had ever met, apart from his father.

That was when the policeman entered the café, looked around, and came over to Josh and Michael.

Five

There's a Law

The policeman was tall and had fierce, black eyebrows. He stood close to Michael and looked intently at him and then into a notebook and then back again. But his voice was quite gentle.

'Stand up, son,' he commanded.

'What's all this about?' Josh asked.

'Please don't interfere, sir.'

Michael slowly stood up.

'Yes,' the policeman said, 'that fits. Height, about five foot four; slight build; hair, reddish-brown; eyes, green; complexion, fair, with freckles. And your name is – let me guess – Michael Chapman?'

'Yes, sir.'

'He hasn't done anything wrong, has he?' Josh asked.

'He has. He's run away from home and his family are very worried. They called us to find him.'

'I only brought him here for the ride,' Josh said. 'I was going to take him back after lunch.'

'Let me have a look at that satchel, Michael,' the

policeman said. Michael handed it over.

'Books,' he said. 'And a sandwich, and clothing, and toilet articles. Are these the things you usually pack when someone asks you out to lunch? Come on, Michael. Let's not waste any more time. I'll take you back. Your family –'

'They're not my family!' Michael exclaimed bitterly. 'The Foxes are horrible to me. What do they want me for?' Seeing the policeman's raised eyebrows, Michael softened his tone. 'Please, sir. Don't make me go back.'

Anna looked worried.

'Couldn't he stay with us until conditions in his home are investigated? Perhaps . . . environment . . . abuse . . . welfare . . . Perhaps,' she suggested.

'Don't *you* start, please,' the policeman said. 'The less you and this gentleman say, the better for you. There's a law against kidnapping.'

'Josh didn't kidnap me! You're right. I did run away. It's all my fault. Josh only gave me a lift. I was hitch-hiking.'

The policeman sighed and put his notebook back in his pocket. 'I know, I know. This sort of thing happens all the time. Let's go, Michael. You needn't worry. Runaways usually get a big welcome when they return home.'

Six

***

A Painful Welcome

As the policeman escorted Michael from the car to his front door, he said, 'They don't allow me to come in this way. I'll have to go around the back.'

'Don't be silly,' the policeman said, smiling. 'I think you're making that up.' He rang the bell.

Mrs Fox opened the door.

'Oh, Michael! My dear boy! I thought something awful had happened to you!'

She seized him with both arms and hugged him tightly to her breast, a gesture of motherly love she had never made before in all the years he had been in her care. Disgusted, Michael wriggled out of her grasp.

'Ugh!' he protested, as if he had tasted a rotten egg.

'He's so shy in front of people he doesn't know. Oh, bless you, officer! I'll never be able to thank you enough for your help.'

'Just doing my job, ma'am. Now, Michael, you be a good boy. You've caused a lot of anxiety and a lot of trouble. You should be grateful that Mrs Fox thinks so much of you and that you have such a fine house to live in. Many children would envy you.'

Mrs Fox stood in the doorway and watched the policeman leave. She smiled, showing lots of teeth, and waved when he turned and gave her a farewell salute before he got into his car and drove away. Then she roughly shoved Michael into the hall and shut the door.

'You beastly little brat!' she snarled. 'You embarrassed me. Go down to your room.'

'There's nothing to eat there. I finished the last few cornflakes and milk and the last two slices of bread.'

'That's just too bad. You should have been here at lunchtime.'

'Why didn't you let me stay away? I met some nice people. They –'

She interrupted him this time by grabbing one of his ears between a tight finger and thumb, making him yelp with pain. She pulled him towards the basement stairs.

'Get down there and stay down till you're called. You'll learn soon enough why we had you brought back. Mr Fox and I have some interesting news for you. He'll tell you about it when he gets home from work.'

'But, Mrs Fox –'

'But nothing. Don't let me see your face till this evening. And you needn't think about escaping again. The basement's outside door is locked and I have the key.'

Michael spent the long, lonely afternoon sitting with a rumbling, empty stomach in the silent, empty kitchen. He thought miserable thoughts about the present and even worse ones about the future. He wondered whether he would ever again feel well-fed and happy. Oh, for a plate piled high with steak and kidney pie! He wished he had gone to school, where, for at least a few hours, he could have forgotten about the Foxes and he had friends to laugh with. He wished he were still with Josh and Anna. He wished he were working on a ranch, doing the things that cowboys do on television. He wished . . . But what was the use of wishing?

At last he heard Mrs Fox's loud, nasal voice ordering him upstairs.

Seven

Mr Fox Shows his Teeth

Mr Fox was lolling back in his customary chair in the kitchen. He was stripped to his greyish T-shirt, drinking beer and smoking one of his stinky cigars.

'Well, if it isn't our wandering boy!' he exclaimed, showing his yellow teeth in a cruel hyena grin. 'Fancy taking off like that without saying goodbye to your beloved guardians – and Cuddles. How ungrateful!'

Cuddles, who had looked up from her special doughnuts and chocolate milk, giggled at her father's wit.

'I only wanted –' Michael tried to explain.

'*You* only wanted!' Mr Fox said, his face turning red with indignation. 'Who cares what you want? You know what you are? You're selfish. What are you?'

Michael just awkwardly stood there.

'Say it,' Mr Fox ordered. 'Say, "I'm selfish".'

'I'm selfish.'

'That's right. You have no consideration for others. You were a nuisance today – a nuisance to me personally. What were you?'

'A nuisance,' Michael said. There was something about Mr Fox's small, red, piggy eyes that frightened him. He didn't want Mr Fox to have one of his temper tantrums. When he did, people sometimes got hurt and things got broken.

'Do you know what you need?' Mr Fox went on.

'No,' Michael replied, wondering what the bully wanted him to say.

'You need a good lesson. Why don't you ask for one?'

'May I have a good lesson?' Michael asked in a small voice.

'You forgot to say please.'

'Please,' Michael said.

'Come closer then.'

Michael reluctantly approached Mr Fox, who smelled like garbage on a hot day. The round-faced man carefully placed his beer bottle on the table.

'Here you are,' he said, chuckling as he swung a big, fat hand. He smacked Michael's face so hard that his ears rattled and he fell over backwards to the floor. He lay there, dazed. His face was stinging. He touched his lower lip with cautious fingertips and felt a trickle of blood.

'Don't lie there,' Mr Fox said. 'Think yourself lucky. That was only a sample of what you'll get if you try to run away again between now and next week. Get up on your feet. Now say you're sorry to Mrs Fox.'

'I won't!' Michael protested. 'You can hit me as much as you like. You can kill me. I don't care. I'm not sorry.'

Mr Fox's face turned even nastier than usual.

'You don't *care*! Well, sonny-boy, I'll soon do something about that!'

Michael scrambled to his feet and walked backwards into a corner. Mr Fox rose unsteadily to his feet. As he moved slowly towards Michael, he heard Cuddles excitedly sniggering.

Mrs Fox surprised Michael by coming between him and her husband.

'That's enough, Charlie,' she said. 'He's not worth wasting your energy on. And if you beat him you'll spoil his nice, clean-cut looks. The agency wouldn't like that, would they?'

What agency? Michael wondered.

'Sit down, Charlie. I'll make you a cup of coffee and you can tell the little brat what we've arranged for him.'

Cuddles excitedly spluttered. 'Yes, Dad. Tell him.'

Eight

The Young Companions Agency

'Running away like that proved to us that we've come to the right decision about you,' Mr Fox told Michael. 'We don't like you. You don't belong here any more. It's time for you to go.'

'Why didn't you let me go, then?' Michael asked.

'There's a right way and a wrong way,' Mr Fox said. 'Your way was the wrong way. Children aren't allowed to travel anywhere they want, any time they want, on their own. You run away like that, sooner or later you're sure to get into trouble with the police. Frankly, it would serve you right. But it would make us look bad. Our way, on the other hand, is the right way.'

Cuddles happily giggled.

'Tell about the agency!' she urged her father.

'I'm coming to that,' he said calmly. He poured beer into his mouth until the bottle was empty. He opened another bottle and took a long puff at his cigar, so that the end glowed red to match the red of his eyes. He coughed wetly and spat into his dirty handkerchief. Michael uneasily shifted from foot to

31

foot. He wished Mr Fox would stop tormenting him and get to the point.

'We thought of sending you to a boarding school,' Mrs Fox said. 'One of those small, private, old-fashioned ones where they still believe in caning boys who break the rules. But even the cheapest would be much too expensive.'

'Who's telling this? Mr Fox irritably demanded.

'You are, dear. I only thought –'

'Don't think. You're not good at it.'

Cuddles pressed a dimpled hand over her mouth to keep in the giggles, but some of them leaked out with a snort through her nose.

'We considered this and that,' Mr Fox continued, 'but *everything* seemed expensive. Why should we waste money on *you*?' he sneered. 'And then, the other day – hey presto! We heard from some people with the perfect answer – the Young Companions Agency.'

'What's that?' Michael asked nervously.

'The Y.C.A. is for children like you,' Mr Fox said. 'Children whose mothers and fathers or guardians are sick of the sight of them.'

Michael sadly looked down at the floor. It is terrible to be hated, even by people like the Foxes.

'It's the latest thing for orphans. Guaranteed one hundred per cent escape-proof. It isn't only a school. It's better than that. And the beauty of it is that I don't have to pay them to take you away. They're going to pay me! They're going to buy you, Michael. Won't that be nice?'

'Buy me? How can they?'

'Because they want to, and we want to sell you.'

32

He smiled at Mrs Fox. 'Don't we, sugarplum?'

'Yes, sweetheart! The sooner, the better!'

'They're sending round one of their vans to collect you on Monday,' Mr Fox told Michael.

'I can hardly wait,' Cuddles said triumphantly.

Nine

Reporting a Crime

Michael did not sleep much that night. When he did, he had frightening dreams about being caught in a huge mousetrap, being kept in a cage in the zoo, and trying to avoid a monster but not being able to move. Awake was even worse, because he felt so helpless.

Maybe Mr Fox's threat to sell Michael to the Young Companions Agency was a cruel joke; but maybe it wasn't. But surely nobody in Britain could sell anybody else. Michael had learnt how people had been taken in chains from Africa in crowded, small sailing ships and sold as slaves in the West Indies and America to do the hard work that very few free people were willing to do. But Britain had abolished the sale of slaves in 1833. Now most people worked for other people for pay, but not if they didn't want to. Nobody had forced Michael to wash neighbours' cars and mow their lawns. He had done so willingly, to earn pocket-money.

If Mr Fox was planning to sell him to the Y.C.A., he was breaking the law. Michael would stop him.

He would telephone the police. He picked up the kitchen telephone and the operator quickly connected him with the police station.

'This is Michael Chapman,' Michael said rather shakily. 'I want to report a crime – a future crime.'

'Oh. A future crime. Where are you calling from?'

Michael gave his address.

'And what is the nature of your prediction?' the sergeant wanted to know.

'There's someone in this house who's planning to go against the Act of Abolition, the law against slavery. His name is Charlie Fox.'

'Just exactly how old are you, Mr Chapman?'

Michael told him.

'It isn't funny to call us with nutty complaints like that,' the sergeant said sternly. 'There are plenty of serious calls about real crimes. Furthermore, at this time of night, you ought to be in bed.'

'Honestly, I need your help. Mr Fox says he's going to sell me on Monday.'

'Obviously, either Mr Fox or you have a weird sense of humour,' the sergeant said wearily. He did not sound even slightly amused. 'Do me a favour, Michael. Go to bed. It's nearly four o'clock in the morning. And don't call us again. I'm warning you. Goodbye.'

Ten

A Kind of Prison

Birds sang as the sun rose. They sounded as if they were enjoying the new day. Michael wasn't. Brushing his teeth, he saw in the mirror above the basin that his lower lip was slightly swollen and bruised. How he hated Mr Fox! Michael supposed he was lucky not to have any broken teeth.

As he was getting dressed, he decided he would get to school early enough to tell his teacher about the Foxes' plan to sell him. She would believe him and know what to do. Charlie Fox had better look out!

Michael heard the basement's inside door open. He went to the kitchen and found Mrs Fox there. She was as ugly as ever, wearing a shiny purple dressing-gown and fluffy purple slippers, with her orange hair in yellow curlers. She was unloading packages and dishes of food from a tray on to the table.

'We mustn't let you starve, must we? The Agency expects you to be in good health on Monday.'

'I phoned the police about you,' Michael said,

hoping to frighten her.

'You did what?' she exclaimed, with an expression of alarm on her face. 'For Heaven's sake, the telephone! I didn't think about the extension down here. You little fool!'

She immediately called the police station and asked for the sergeant on duty.

'I want to apologise,' she said in the phony, sweet voice she used when speaking to strangers. 'I'm afraid my son phoned the station in the middle of the night and said some silly things. He's a very . . . imaginative child. He believes in flying saucers. You know what children are like.'

The sergeant asked for the boy's name and she gave it.

'There's nothing here in the book,' the sergeant said. 'Evidently the night man didn't bother to log the call. We get a lot of calls from crazies late at night. You can forget about it. We won't be taking any action.'

'Oh, thank you, sergeant. You're very under-standing. I'll make sure that nothing like that ever happens again.'

'I'm not your son,' Michael said, as soon as Mrs Fox had hung up.

'Thank goodness for that. You're a pest. You might have ruined everything. Well, there won't be any more phone calls.'

So saying, she jerked the telephone plug from the wall and put the telephone on the tray to take upstairs.

'There are other ways,' he muttered. She heard him.

'Are there? Of course, you think you can tell someone at school. Wrong. From now on, you aren't going to school. I'm going to phone and say the doctor has ordered you to stay at home. No school. You aren't going anywhere. You can't climb out of the windows because of the bars. I'm disconnecting the stove and removing the matches so you can't start a fire. And even if you could, you wouldn't want to destroy your daddy's precious house, would you? And yourself? No, Michael, you're stuck until we let you go.'

He felt hot tears beginning to fill his eyes, but he would not let her see him cry. He said nothing. She went away, and he soon heard the key turn in the lock of the door at the top of the stairs.

He was in a kind of prison.

He couldn't think of anything to do. He just sat there. Now he was sure the Foxes meant what they said.

He wondered what would happen on Monday, and, of course, he worried.

Eleven

Out of the Frying Pan . . .

Early on Monday morning, Mrs Fox unlocked the basement door.

'Never mind about finishing your cornflakes. The van's here. We don't want to keep the man waiting.'

'I haven't packed,' Michael said.

'You don't have to pack. The agency says they'll provide everything you'll need.'

'Let me take a few of my favourite books and compact discs, Mrs Fox. Please.'

'They want you as you are. Cuddles will keep any records and books she likes. We'll get rid of the rest. Come on!'

'But –'

'But nothing. Do I have to lead you by the ear?'

Michael followed her upstairs and out of the front door.

A gleaming, new-looking van was parked in front of the house – pale blue, with a dark blue crest and the agency's initials on the side. A young man in a dark blue uniform, with a chauffeur's cap, was standing by the kerb.

'Good morning, Michael,' he said, touching the peak of his cap in a friendly salute.

'Don't forget the money,' Mrs Fox reminded the chauffeur.

'Of course not, Mrs Fox,' he politely assured her. 'I have it right here.' He handed her a bulky envelope. She eagerly ripped it open and started counting fifty-pound bank-notes. Michael wondered how much had been paid for him. Did somebody think he was worth a lot? Should he try to escape? He knew he wouldn't get far, so he stayed.

'I have a camera with me,' the chauffeur said. 'Sometimes the adults and children like to have photographs of the farewell scene – kissing each other goodbye or shaking hands. The pictures make nice souvenirs. Would you –'

'It's all here,' Mrs Fox said, stuffing the wad of money back into the envelope.

'No photographs, thank you,' Michael said.

'I understand,' the young man said.

Without further ado, Mrs Fox returned to the house.

The young man drove away smoothly, soon reaching the motorway. He speeded along then, eastwards between green embankments and trees in full leaf. Here and there cherry trees still blossomed, pink and white, bright in the sunshine.

'A splendid day for cricket,' the chauffeur commented.

Michael was not in a playful mood.

'Where are you taking me?'

40

'To the home.'

'Where's that?'

'Sorry, Michael. The location is secret. In fact at the next convenient stopping-place we'll have to put on your blindfold.'

Michael was very glad to be getting away from the Foxes, even though he was being banished from his own home. But where was he going? And what would happen when he got there? Out of the frying pan, into the fire?

The driver was quite pleasant so when they stopped and Michael had a black mask without eye-holes tied to his face he was not *very* frightened.

'It won't be for long,' the driver said. 'We'll get where we're going in less than an hour. Don't ask me any more questions because I'm not allowed to answer any. Mr Poindexter, our director, will receive you and tell you all you need to know.'

In the total darkness of the blindfold, Michael had no sense of direction. However, he did notice that now there were no sounds of traffic. He thought he might be imagining things but be believed he could smell the sea.

Then the tyres crunched gravel. The van stopped. The engine was switched off.

'Welcome to the Y.C.A.,' the driver said, as he removed the blindfold.

Michael found that he was at the main entrance of a large, square building that appeared to be made almost entirely of black mirror, like a modern skyscraper in Dallas. Beyond it, there were an extensive, well-kept lawn, a barbed-wire fence, a beach and the sea. A breeze made small waves.

There were no other buildings in sight.

'A splendid day for swimming,' the driver said. But Michael felt too nervous to reply.

'You'll feel better when Mr Poindexter explains the way we operate,' the driver promised, guiding Michael into the marble lobby. 'Michael Chapman,' he told a woman at a desk marked RECEPTION.

'Good,' she said. 'Mr Poindexter was enquiring about him. Michael is to go right up.'

Twelve

Mr Poindexter's Computer

When Michael timidly entered a big, luxurious office on the top floor, Mr Poindexter, a thin man with grey hair and a pale, greyish face, wearing a black suit, a white shirt and a grey tie, was sitting at the black desk. The whole room and everything in it were black or grey or white. He was peering through his glasses closely at the screen of a computer, whispering to himself (or perhaps to the computer), as his bony fingers worked rapidly on the keyboard.

'Good. Good. Most satisfactory,' he said.

Hearing Michael utter a nervous little cough, the director sat up straight and turned to face him.

'Michael Chapman!' Mr Poindexter said.

'Yes, sir,' Michael replied gloomily.

'Cheer up! You're a very lucky boy!'

Lucky? Michael only raised his eyebrows in astonishment. He didn't feel very lucky. His mother and father were dead. His so-called guardians, the Foxes, had been horrid to him in every way. He had tried to escape from them; the police had caught him and taken him back, and the Foxes had become even worse than before. And now he was in the hands of strangers in a strange place, and he had no idea how they would treat him. How could he have been less lucky?

'We, at the Young Companions Agency, are choosy,' Mr Poindexter said proudly. 'We don't take just any children. We have well-qualified investigators all over the United Kingdom, everywhere from Land's End to John O'Groat's and from the North Sea to the Irish Sea, constantly in search of suitable boys and girls. All children may be considered, but, of course, there are some adults who, for reasons of their own, are not willing to part with them, even though we pay so well – I mean, have so much to offer. The Agency, on the other hand, refuses some children. We will take only the best sorts – healthy, pleasant-looking, intelligent, likeable children who enjoy games – whom, we know, we can easily place.'

Mr Poindexter approvingly patted the top of his computer, as one might pat a beloved dog.

'You have been in my computer ever since your father passed away, Michael. One of our investigators has had you under observation every day since then, has questioned many of the persons who know you, and has sent us a great deal of information about you, almost all to your credit, I am happy to say.'

The director smiled.

'We have been especially favourably impressed by evidence of your popularity at school. You had many friends there. Our investigator sent us

44

photographs and tape-recordings of all of you.'

Michael thought it was spooky that people could sneak up on other people and find out a lot of private facts and opinions about them in these secret ways.

'Our investigator sent a complimentary report on your brave attempt to get away from home. And, naturally, it was he who first telephoned the police to tell them you were to be found with Mr and Mrs Driscoll – Josh and Anna. We didn't want to lose you, Michael. Our man, while pretending to be an ordinary diner at the café, was able to ask Mrs Driscoll a few questions. He learned that she and her husband had taken a liking to you. That's another point to your credit. I've been reviewing your case in depth,' the director said, again patting his faithful computer, 'and I'm very pleased we have been able to get you.'

Indignation made Michael forget to be frightened.

'But it's wrong to buy children like this. I'm not a slave and I'm not a thing.'

'Really, Michael!' Mr Poindexter cheerfully objected. 'Of course you're not a slave. What an idea! Who said you were?'

'Mrs Fox said you paid for me. I saw Mrs Fox count the money.'

'Perhaps nobody has yet explained about our . . . arrangement. The Agency didn't pay for you, yourself. We paid for a contract for your services. We'll keep that contract until we, in turn, provide your services to someone else. We won't be selling *you*, Michael. We'll be selling your *services*. Grown-

45

ups do business like that every day. There's nothing wrong.'

Mr Poindexter might think there was nothing wrong, but Michael did. He wondered how Mr Poindexter would feel if Michael sold Mr Poindexter's services. And what services would Michael be made to perform anyway? His teacher had told the class that children used to be forced to do many hard jobs, hauling wagonloads of coal in underground mines or climbing up inside chimneys to sweep out the soot.

'Don't look so miserable, Michael,' the director said. 'If you want to succeed these days, you have to look happy. That's one of the first rules. Let me assure you that you're exactly the kind of child we're always looking for. It'll take very little time to prepare you for your next move. I'm glad to say we have already been able to arrange your first assignment, thanks to one of our enterprising salespersons.

'Michael,' he announced in a grand voice, 'we are sending you to a very distinguished client, Lady ffrith-Ponsonby of Nether Pining-in-Marsh, Gloucestershire. I'm sure you'll do very well there.'

Thirteen

Mumsy and Mikey-Wikey

One morning a few days later, after some physical and intelligence tests and a neat haircut, Michael was awakened a little earlier than usual by a guard unlocking his bedroom door.

'Today's the day, Michael,' the guard said. 'The director said you should wear these new clothes.' He placed a cardboard box on the bed. 'You'd better make it snappy in the shower. A limousine will be ready to take you right after breakfast.'

Michael looked out through the small, barred window and saw that the sky was blue. Though he was anxious about the future, he was impatient to go.

Dressed in a blue shirt, blue jeans and white tennis shoes and carrying his toilet things in a new case, Michael was driven away in a long, black Rolls-Royce. It reminded him of pictures of the Queen leaving Buckingham Palace.

During the journey, there was no conversation. He was alone in cushioned silence in the back, and the glass partition between him and the driver was closed.

Michael looked out. They sped smoothly along motorways and then narrower roads through small towns and villages and between trees and fields, turned on to winding lanes, through an old stone gateway, and up an avenue of beech trees, to a large house of faded orange bricks and greyish-yellowish Cotswold stone, Pining Manor.

The chauffeur left and a maid took Michael to her ladyship. She was in the conservatory, a glass-enclosed room full of small palm trees and flowers, having her elevenses at a round glass and wrought-iron table. She was a rather fat old woman with white hair, gold-rimmed spectacles, a long, purple velvet dress with a white lace collar and a lot of diamonds. At her feet sat a fluffy white cat with yellow eyes, who looked up crossly at Michael as if he were a burglar.

'Good morning, Lady ffrith-Ponsonby,' he said politely, as he had been instructed.

'Hello, dear boy,' she replied with a loving smile that deepened the creases in her cheeks and chins. She took his hand and warmly squeezed it. 'No formality here. You must call me Mumsy.'

He blushed with embarrassment but obediently nodded.

'I'm having hot chocolate,' she said, pressing a bell-push for her maid. 'D'you like drinking chocolate?'

'Oh, yes.'

'Yes, what?'

'Yes, please,' Michael said.

'Yes, please *what?*' she urged him.

'Yes, please, Mumsy.'

He felt very silly. Lady ffrith-Ponsonby looked old enough to be his great-grandmother.

'Come here,' she said in a coaxing voice.

He stepped forward.

'Closer,' she said.

He approached so near to her chair that she was able to put her fat arms around him. She was surprisingly strong and pulled him forward, off balance, until she could cover his face with fat, wet kisses. She smelled so sweet that he was afraid she would suffocate him.

'There,' she said with a soppy smile as she let him go. 'Welcome to Pining Manor. I feel sure you're going to make your Mumsy very, very happy.'

The maid arrived.

'Yes, my lady?' she asked.

'Another cup of chocolate. Lots of whipped cream for darling little Mikey-Wikey. And a plateful of chocolate éclairs. Have you ever had choc éclairs?' she enquired with a merry twinkle.

'No, I haven't,' Michael admitted.

'Oh, Mikey-Wikey. You'll adore them. All good little boys adore chocky creamies.'

The cat, whose worst fears had already been justified, got to his feet and, with slow dignity, walked from the room.

'Look at the naughty thing!' Lady ffrith-Ponsonby exclaimed with a wheezy puff of laughter. 'I do believe Percival is jealous. He always is when I have a pretty, young guest.'

Pretty! Michael thought he was an ordinary boy. He had never before been called pretty – or, for that matter, Mikey-Wikey. Had he fallen into the clutches of a nut case?

Michael's bedroom suite had been specially decorated and furnished for him. It was like an infant's nursery. There was a big cot with wooden-barred sides. On a sofa sat the stuffed woolly figures of Winnie the Pooh and his friends. Mother Goose figures colourfully brightened the pale-blue wallpaper: Mary had a little lamb; Little Jack Horner sat in the corner, eating his Christmas pie; the little dog laughed to see such fun; and Michael squirmed with indignation.

There was worse to come. The next morning he found that, instead of his shirt and jeans, an absurdly ornamental costume had been carefully laid out. Apparently, he was expected to wear a floppy yellow silk bow-tie, a yellow silk suit with knee-length pantaloons, yellow stockings and orange patent-leather shoes with golden buckles.

Wearing these extraordinary things, Michael looked at himself in the mirror. He decided that he must take desperate emergency action. He could not allow that mad old woman – his owner? – to treat him like some sort of live baby-doll. He began to undress . . .

A few minutes later, he went downstairs to breakfast, absolutely stark naked.

Lady ffrith-Ponsonby uttered a shrill scream, and her spectacles fell off her nose and into her porridge.

'Mikey, pet,' she feebly protested, when she was again able to speak. 'Haven't you forgotten something?'

'Someone took my clothes,' he explained.

'But –'

'You can use the yellow silk to make pyjamas for the cat. I've torn the suit into small strips.'

Within a couple of hours, Michael, wearing his shirt, jeans and tennis shoes, was in the agency Rolls-Royce, returning to Mr Poindexter.

Fourteen

The Human Cannonball

'Mr Poindexter wants to see you,' Michael was told early the next day.

On the way to the director's office, he felt sure that there was going to be trouble. He certainly had misbehaved at Pining Manor, and Lady ffrith-Ponsonby had reason to complain. But Mr Poindexter gave him a friendly smile.

'Well, Michael, that didn't take long, did it?'

'I'm sorry, Mr Poindexter. She –'

'Sorry? There's nothing to be sorry about. We never give clients their money back if they don't like our children. That's part of the agreement; the gamble is theirs. Now, let me see what your next assignment is going to be.'

The director turned to his computer, while Michael stood by the desk and nervously twisted his fingers together.

'Ah, Satellite TV . . .'

At the television company office in London, Buddy Da Silva, the famous producer, took the big cigar

52

out of his mouth and explained Michael's role in a new show, *Satellite Circus*.

'You're our new stunt boy.'

'What's that, Mr Da Silva?' Michael asked.

'Don't worry. The director will tell you what to do. You look right – ginger hair: good; we won't have to dye it. Rod Wayne, the boy star you'll be standing in for, has auburn hair almost exactly the same colour. You're feeling OK, huh? Mr Poindexter assures us you're quite an athlete. You ain't scared of heights, I hope. No?'

'No,' Michael said, wondering why the man wanted to know.

Mr Da Silva chuckled and patted Michael on the back.

'It won't be as tough as you figure. We'll use a guaranteed safety net. And just in case, you'll be fully insured.'

'Just in case what?' Michael wondered.

'You'll do great,' Mr Da Silva promised.

A huge warehouse had been fixed up to look like the centre ring of a circus, surrounded by many rows of seats, which were now fully occupied by an audience who had been let in free. Television cameras and cameramen and batteries of floodlights were mounted on raised platforms on all sides of the ring. At one end of the building a net was suspended close to the concrete floor and, at the opposite end, there was a large, silver-grey steel cannon.

Michael was dressed in tight red overalls and red boots.

'Hi, Mike!' said a man wearing a sunhelmet, sunglasses, a bush-jacket and corduroy trousers. 'I'm Herman Glitz, the director. Welcome to *Satellite Circus*. I bet millions of kids would give anything to be in your place today. I want you to meet Rod Wayne. He's going to be a very big star when this show goes out world-wide.'

A pale-faced boy the same size as Michael and wearing the same sort of red overalls and boots grinned and casually saluted.

'Hi, man,' Rod said. 'Here's hoping things go better today. Yesterday was a mess.'

'All right, all right, Mike. That's only Rod's little joke. He has a terrific sense of humour. There's nothing to worry about here. We're filming the whole thing, so if we have any problems the first time . . . Well, we can just do it again.'

'What –' Michael began to ask.

'Rod's very sensitive,' Mr Glitz said. 'He's an artist, you understand. This shot-out-of-a-cannon bit is the climax of our story, Mike, but Rod is kind of allergic to heights –'

'And big bangs,' Rod added, 'and flying without wings, and sudden stops, if you know what I mean.'

'So that's where you come in, Mike,' the director cheerfully pointed out. 'The stunt boy. It's a very important responsibility. For a few seconds, *Satellite Circus* will depend entirely on you.'

'You mean –' Michael began.

'All we do is this,' the director said. 'Rod walks to the foot of the ladder, where we shoot a close-up of his face. You know, showing him looking brave. We stop the cameras. Rod gets away, and you take his place. You don't have to say any lines or anything like that. All you have to do is climb up the ladder to the cannon. You'll be helped into the breech, facing up the barrel. Boom! The next thing you know, you're in the safety net and everyone's cheering. Then, of course, Rod takes over again. It's simple.'

'I don't think I like that idea,' Michael said. 'What happened yesterday?'

'Oh, boy!' Rod exclaimed. 'You –'

But Mr Glitz interrupted him with an impatient frown.

'Rod's only kidding, everything's been carefully checked. So let's get going.'

'I don't want to do it,' Michael said.

' "Want" doesn't come into it,' the director said firmly. 'Your agency has charged us plenty for you. There's a lot of money involved. There's no time for "want" or "don't want".'

Without further ado, the director hustled Michael over to the foot of the ladder. After Rod had been photographed posing as a fearless human cannonball, Michael climbed up the ladder to the cannon platform.

Two men in black overalls helped Michael to wriggle through the breech into the close-fitting, dark, oily barrel. Lying face-down with his arms stretched forward, he heard the small, heavy round door slam behind him and a bolt click shut.

Waiting was the worst part. The seconds seemed like hours. Then, suddenly –

POW!!!

After the first violent shock, Michael shot up and

up and over and down and down and
   BOUNCED and **bounced** and bounced
   up and down and up and down
   in the strong, flexible net . . .

The audience cheered loud and long, as they had been requested. And Rod, smiling proudly, stood on the ground and repeatedly bowed.

'Terrific!' Mr Glitz said, back in the dressing-room, as Rod and Michael changed into their ordinary clothes.

Michael felt excited and pleased.

'Did you like the way I waved to the crowd?' Rod asked the director.

'Yeah, Rod. That was a nice touch. You were perfect.'

'What do I have to do tomorrow?' Michael wanted to know.

'Tomorrow?' Mr Glitz echoed in surprise. 'I don't care *what* you do tomorrow. We only bought you as stunt boy for one day. Your car is outside to take you back.'

Fifteen

Perfectly Yucky

'You did well, Michael,' Mr Poindexter said, smiling contentedly as he thought of all the money that Michael was bringing in. 'Now we've got another exciting TV assignment for you.'

'Not stunt boy again?' Michael asked anxiously.

Mr Poindexter smiled some more.

'It's really more of a comedy assignment. They promise it's going to be a lot of laughs.'

An agency chauffeur drove Michael to a big, famous television building in West London.

'I've been ordered to stay and keep an eye on you, Michael, so don't get any clever ideas about running away. But why would you want to? What kid wouldn't want to be on telly?'

As they crossed the high-ceilinged lobby, Michael saw a smart lady known in almost every home in Britain for wearing different clothes every day and for being able to read the news in a friendly voice, without looking at all upset, even when the news was terrible.

'Help me!' Michael said, as she walked past.

'Sorry, mate,' she replied. 'No time for autographs. I got a broadcast to do.'

She headed quickly towards the lifts, and the chauffeur gave Michael a painful prod in the ribs with a sharp elbow.

'None of that, Michael,' the chauffeur said.

A woman at the reception desk directed them to a studio on an upper floor.

Going up in the lift, Michael wondered whether he'd have to recite a lot of words in front of the cameras. He had never acted at school, unless he counted playing one of the shepherds in a Nativity play in kindergarten. All he'd had to do was to sing carols, which he'd enjoyed.

When they reached the studio, things happened bewilderingly fast.

'Wardrobe wants you,' a young man told Michael. 'And hurry. You're nearly five minutes late. We have a schedule here.'

In a dressing-room, Michael was quickly dressed as a footballer, in a red-and-white-striped jersey, white shorts, red stockings and black-and-white boots.

'Come on!' another man urged him. 'Make-up's waiting!'

In a room like a hairdressing salon, with a row of swivel chairs close to washbasins and brightly lighted mirrors, a woman quickly shampooed his hair and fluffed it up with a blow-dryer and arranged it in soft waves, with a lock of hair down over one eye.

'Lovely!' the hairdresser said, admiring her work. 'Just *adorable*!'

'What's this play about?' Michael enquired uneasily. He couldn't imagine a story about an adorable soccer hero.

'You're really lucky,' she said. 'You're going to star in the first of an important new series of Fizzo commercials.'

Fizzo is Britain's Number One detergent. By now, you must have heard the Fizzo song about a million times: 'Gee-whizzo! Get new Fizzo! Fizzo fizzes colours brighter! Fizzo fizzes whites much whiter! Fizzo –' You probably don't need reminding that Fizzo chemists have developed new, smaller, foamier bubbles that make all fabrics Fizzo-fresh.

Fizzo is soap.

Even disgusting Mrs Fox always had an easily recognizable red-and-white box of Fizzo in the laundry-room, though she had used the room so little, and cleaned it so much less, since the death of Michael's father. Now spiders were using the room to spin some of their best flytraps, and mice had made a nest in a crumpled heap of used towels that had been thrown into a corner.

But anyway . . . Fizzo commercials are shown on television more times a day than any other commercials. Michael was supposed to feel honoured to be in one.

A make-up woman powder-puffed Michael's face suntan orange, darkened his eyebrows with a grease-paint pencil, and made his lips rosy pink with a lipstick brush.

'Perfect!' she said happily. Perfectly yucky, he thought.

He was ready for action.

And what action!

First, pictures were taken showing him looking 'lovely', 'adorable' and 'perfect', in his clean football uniform, while an actress wearing an apron, pretending to be his mother, admired him in her kitchen. Those were the 'before' pictures. They were also the 'after' pictures, showing how 'lovely', 'adorable' and 'perfect' he looked after his soiled uniform had been whirled around in a washing-machine with Fizzo.

'I thought we'd never get his things clean,' his 'mother' exclaimed. 'Thank heaven for Fizzo's magic bubbles! Fizzo has made his clothes like new again!'

Next came the bit that they said was going to be a lot of laughs. Pictures had to be taken to show Michael getting very, very dirty. Those were to be the 'between' pictures, to show that nothing was too dirty for Fizzo.

For those, Michael was taken to a part of the studio that had become a small section of a football field – an unusually muddy one.

'You stand there, Michael, in front of the goal,' the director said. 'That's it.' He turned to an assistant and commanded him to, 'Switch on the rain!'

From overhead pipes, cold water gushed down on Michael's head.

'Good,' the director said. 'All right, kick the ball at him!'

A professional striker beside the camera kicked a football at Michael as hard as possible. He caught it in front of his chest and it almost knocked him down. The ball stung his hands.

'Cut!' the director shouted. 'That's no good, Michael. You're supposed to fall down.'

'A goalkeeper should be wearing gloves,' Michael said.

'I'm the director,' the director said. 'You follow my directions. I don't want gloves. This is a kids' game, understand? Now, we'll try that again. This time, when you catch the ball, I want you to slip over backwards and sit in the mud with a surprised look on your face. OK?'

After the backwards slip, the director ordered a frontwards slip ('All the way, Michael – right down; your face in the mud; that's the biggest laugh'), and slips to one side and the other. Eventually, Michael was soaking wet and thickly covered in mud from head to foot.

'Great!' the director said. 'We've got all we need. Somebody take the boy away.'

Michael's hands were cold and red and sore and he had bruises all over his body, where the football had hit him, again and again.

'Sorry, Michael,' the professional striker said. 'That's what we're being paid for.'

'Come on, Michael,' said the chauffeur, who was really quite sympathetic deep down. 'Let's go home.'

'Can't I have a bath?' Michael protested.

'Not here, you can't,' the director said. 'We don't want you messing up our dressing-rooms.'

'What about the football clothes?' Michael said.

'You can keep them as a souvenir,' the director replied, and he and his crew laughed.

The chauffeur spread newspapers on the back seat of the limousine, so that Michael wouldn't soil the upholstery.

A short time later, when the Fizzo commercial was first broadcast, Mr and Mrs Fox and their fat daughter recognized Michael.

'Coo!' Cuddles said. She had mixed feelings. She enjoyed watching Michael falling about in the rain and the mud, but then she said, 'I wonder what they're paying him for that?'

'Whatever it is,' Mrs Fox said, 'he ought to give us some.' Mr Fox grunted in agreement.

'If it hadn't been for us, he wouldn't have gone to that agency, would he?'

The commercial was shown over and over again. One evening, Josh and Anna Driscoll saw it.

'That's our friend Michael,' Josh said.

'Poor Michael!' Anna said.

'Nobody could like doing that. Somebody must be forcing him to do it, for the money. I'm going to find out who.'

Josh had a difficult search ahead of him.

Sixteen

The Palace of Pelf

Several weeks went by. Michael began to fear that he was helplessly stuck in his terrible situation. He had never before realised how many silly, selfish and unkind people there are in the world. But, of course, nice people would never have thought of buying his services, would they? It turned out that he was wrong about that.

When he was urgently summoned to report to Mr Poindexter's office, Michael wondered what it could be this time? Would he be able to enjoy anything like a normal family life ever again? It did not seem likely.

'One of our senior staff has received a most important request,' Mr Poindexter said in his most solemn manner. 'Michael, have we got a deal for you! It's probably the biggest deal we've made since I established the agency. You – your services – have been bought by the richest kid in Britain.'

The journey in the limousine was even longer than usual. At last, the Rolls-Royce stopped at a high granite wall deep in woodland. When the gilded black iron gates swung open, they drove up a long, private driveway between trees and fields and lawns and flower-gardens and fountains in ornamental ponds and came, eventually, to a towering red-brick mansion with dozens of chimneys and hundreds of windows. A veritable palace, with wide, stone steps leading up to marble pillars beside immense double doors.

Above the bell-push there was a golden plaque engraved with a very famous name, FLEETWOOD PELF. He was known everywhere as the richest man in Britain. He was the founder and chairman of Consolidated Universal Associates, the world's biggest manufacturers of the world's most expensive products, all very high-tech. They were:

BOMBS
ROCKETS
GROUND-TO-AIR MISSILES
AIR-TO-GROUND MISSILES
AIR-TO-AIR MISSILES
ANTI-MISSILE MISSILES
ANTI-ANTI-MISSILE MISSILES

and all other weapons, devices, explosives and poisons that people all over the world buy in vast quantities in case they decide to kill each other.

'Michael Chapman's here,' the chauffeur announced into the intercom.

There was a *beep*, and a door opened.

A uniformed guard wearing a gun in a holster led Michael to the office of the building manager, who took him to the butler, who took him to the governess in charge of Fleetwood Pelf II, Fleetwood

Pelf's only child and the heir to the Pelf billions.

'Here he is, Miss Borax,' said the butler.

'And about time, too, if I may say so. Master Fleetwood is becoming very impatient.'

'We will be as quick as we can, Mr Wodehouse,' said Miss Borax, a large lady with a grey top-knot and a round face, whose body appeared to be made of beige cushions. 'But hygiene first!'

In a changing-room, Michael had to strip off his new clothes, which were immediately thrown into a disposal bin. He was ordered to take a bath in steaming water that smelled like a hospital. Then he was given a new outfit of clothes, including shorts like the ones he wore at school for gym.

When he emerged from the changing room, Miss Borax said, 'Dr Scalpell will see you now.'

In a brightly-lit clinic, a doctor carefully examined Michael from head to foot, outside and inside.

'He's in good shape,' Dr Scalpell finally announced. 'He's clear to go to Master Fleetwood.'

Seventeen

The Richest Kid

'Go in through that door,' Miss Borax told Michael, after a long walk along polished corridors. 'I'll leave you here. I have some things to do in another part of the house.'

Michael opened the door and went in and was hit in the face by a big cream-pie – *splat*! The cream was thick and soft, covering him from his forehead to his chin.

'Ha!' yelled a boy whom Michael could not yet see, because his eyes had cream all over them. 'Got you!' The boy laughed and laughed, as Michael picked the sticky mess from his eyelids and nose and mouth, puffing and blowing so that he could breathe properly.

'Ugh! Ooh! Eeyuck!' were the only sounds Michael uttered at first.

'What's the matter?' the boy asked, between giggles. 'Don't you like banana? What flavour *do* you like?'

Now Michael could see. Fleetwood was a boy about Michael's own age and size. Fleetwood's hair was brown and curly. He had quite a nice face, really. He was wearing a yellow jogging suit with the initials FP embroidered in white on the breast pocket.

'You do look silly!' Fleetwood said.

'You'd look silly if I threw a pie in your face,' Michael said. 'Miss Borax just gave me these clothes and look at them!'

'Don't call anything about me silly,' Fleetwood said with a scowl. 'I'm the one who says when something's silly. You are *my* companion – mine – and you have to agree with whatever I want. Understand?'

'And if you throw a pie in my face, what am I supposed to do?'

'That was a joke. What do you think you're supposed to do when someone makes a joke? Haven't you got a sense of humour?'

'A pie-in-the-face joke isn't very funny if it's your face,' Michael pointed out.

'A joke is a joke,' Fleetwood insisted. 'Here, shake hands. No hard feelings. We're going to be spending a lot of time together.'

Fleetwood offered his right hand. When Michael grasped it, he felt the vibrant sizzle of one of those wind-up trick buzzers, like an electric shock, in the palm of his hand.

'Ouch!' Michael yelped, jerking his hand away agitatedly.

'Ha, ha!' Fleetwood laughed triumphantly. 'You have to be a sport. It's been a real drag around here with nobody to play with. I'm going to make up for lost time. I want to have fun.'

Michael frowned.

'There's a place where you can wash,' Fleetwood said. 'Over there behind the soda-fountain.'

'Right,' Michael said. 'I'd better get cleaned up. Miss Borax seems strict about cleanness.'

'You needn't do anything because of *her*,' Fleetwood said scornfully. He had a loud, boastful way of speaking. 'I could easily have her fired. I can have anything I want, and do anything I want, and don't forget it.'

'OK,' Michael said. 'I'll clean up because *you* say so.'

Fleetwood called after him: 'Use the pink soap!'

When Michael worked up a lather with the pink soap it turned dark green, staining his hands. He had to scrub them with a bar of ordinary white soap to get them back to normal. Michael gritted his teeth to keep calm. After a while, he succeeded in removing all the cream, even from inside his ears.

'What kept you so long?' Fleetwood enquired when Michael returned. 'I want to show you some of my things.'

'I'm ready,' Michael said. He glanced around the spacious playroom. Opposite the soda-fountain there were a row of picture-windows and a couple of glass doors. The shiny marble floor in between was crowded with video games and other amusement machines and gymnastic equipment.

'I have just about everything that money can buy,' Fleetwood said, 'and more. The engineers in Dad's Research and Development Department keep inventing new recreational gadgets for me. My dad's the richest man in Britain.'

'Yes, I've heard of him,' Michael said.

'Everyone's heard of him. He's always in the news on television and on the covers of magazines and the front pages of newspapers, usually with a king, sheikh, president, prime minister or leader of industry.'

'But never with his family,' Michael said.

'My dad makes more money than all the stars in Hollywood and all the pro-golfers and tennis players put together. He owns banks all over the world. Every minute of every day and night he becomes many pounds richer – pounds, dollars, yen, Deutschmarks, francs and any other foreign money you can think of. My dad has his own planes and helicopters and the biggest yacht in the world. My dad is super-rich.'

Fleetwood paused for a moment to catch his breath and wait for Michael to look impressed. Michael tried hard not to.

'I bet you can't guess what my allowance is,' Fleetwood said. Michael thought of the very few pounds that he himself had earned and how little he had been able to buy.

'Twenty pounds a week?' he ventured.

Fleetwood laughed.

'I haven't got an allowance. I can spend as much as I like. I have every gold and platinum credit card you ever heard of. I can phone all over the world and give my name and people send me everything I ask for . . .'

As Fleetwood went on and on, Michael's mind went temporarily blank. When he started paying attention again, Fleetwood was still saying 'I' this, 'I' that and 'I' the other thing – 'I . . . I . . . I . . .'

Eighteen

How to Win at Snooker

Fleetwood stopped the catalogue and showed off some of his high-tech fun-aids.

There was an electronic see-saw which one child could ride by himself.

'That's one game I don't need you for,' Fleetwood said with a self-satisfied smile. Michael wondered how anyone could enjoy riding on a see-saw alone.

'Here's my electronic slide,' Fleetwood said, pointing to a spiral tower extending all the way from the floor to the high ceiling. 'See, there's a moving stairway at the back, so you can get to the top without climbing.'

There was an electronic no-push swing.

'This is my electronic bicycle, with video, all you have to do is sit on it. The motorised pedals automatically move your feet around, and on this wide screen there's a colour movie of beautiful scenery on a sunny day. There's a selector console on the handle-bars – see: you can change the movie at the press of a button to show what it would be like riding a bicycle anywhere in the world.'

At one end of the playroom, they came to an enormous parcel.

'It must have been delivered this morning; new stuff keeps coming in every day. Let's see what they've sent me now. Help me unwrap it.'

Michael was not surprised that Fleetwood did not believe in saying 'please'.

'Is unwrapping parcels part of my job?' Michael asked.

'Your job is to do what I tell you to do. If I say, "Stand on your head," you stand on your head. You're my companion.'

'I thought companions were always equal and nice to each other.'

'Well, think again. You're my unequal companion. Come on, Michael. Let's start unwrapping.'

They tore off the brown paper and cardboard and gradually revealed a full-sized snooker table.

'I remember. I ordered this yesterday. It was supposed to arrive last night. This is no ordinary snooker table. It's special.' He chuckled. 'Do you know how to play snooker?'

'No, I'm sorry, I don't. But I've seen it played on television.'

'I'll show you how.'

And he did.

Michael quickly learned how to hold the cue, how to aim one ball to hit another to try to make it roll into one of the pockets, the six holes at the sides and corners of the large, green-baize-covered table.

The only trouble was that no matter how

71

carefully Michael aimed he could never make a ball go into a pocket. But Fleetwood always kept getting the balls in, even when he didn't seem to be trying, until every one had gone and he had won.

Once again, Fleetwood laughed.

'This is a specially-made *magnetic* snooker table. There's a secret switch here, under the edge of the table. When it's your turn, I press the switch a certain way, so the pockets are negative. They force the balls away – they're special balls with metal in them. You can't get them in, no matter how straight you aim. When it's my turn I press the switch the other way, so the pockets are positive. Their magnets attract the metal inside the balls, kind of suck them in. Even if my aim's a little crooked, every shot's a winner. Do you understand?'

'But that's cheating! What's the fun in playing a game you can't possibly lose?'

'I like winning. Losing's what you're for. When we play chess or draughts, I'll be the player with the computer on my side. I can programme the computer so it'll be impossible for you to beat me. You don't expect me to let *you* win, do you?'

Nineteen

Getting to Know Fleetwood

It was lunchtime.

Fleetwood and Michael sat at opposite ends of a long table in Fleetwood's luxurious private dining room.

'What'll you have?' Fleetwood asked.

'What *can* I have?' Michael asked back.

'Anything you like. I have my own chef, who used to cook at the Ritz-Balmoral Hotel. He has huge deep-freezes in the store-rooms behind the kitchen. There are all the regular dishes, such as steak and lobster. I sometimes get bored with stuff like that, but there are all kinds of fancy things as well – wild boar, octopus, hummingbird tongues and so on. Name it; I've got it.'

Fleetwood boasts even about food, Michael thought. He sighed, thinking of the Driscolls in the café.

'Could I have steak and kidney pie, please?' he said.

Fleetwood shrugged his shoulders at this unexpected request.

'I suppose so. Why not?'

A waiter brought what they ordered, steak and kidney pie for Michael and grilled paw of chimpanzee with pineapple sauce for Fleetwood. The steak and kidney pie was delicious, and Fleetwood was envious of Michael's obvious enjoyment of it. Fleetwood just played around with the mess on his plate. They both had chocolate ice-cream for dessert.

'Why don't you eat your meals with your father and mother?' Michael wanted to know. He thought Fleetwood was lucky to have a father and mother.

Fleetwood looked surprised.

'Dad's abroad, on business. He's in Arabia this week, I think. Or maybe that was last week. I know he's either in Arabia or Japan. He spends most of the time travelling. Weapons and all those things are very expensive these days, he says. He has to spend more and more time abroad persuading people to buy the latest inventions. Sometimes he has to lend them the money to buy what he's selling.'

'What about your mother?' Michael asked.

Fleetwood's eyes moistened.

'She's in bed.'

'Oh, I'm sorry,' Michael said.

'There's nothing wrong with her. She's not *ill*. But she doesn't feel very well early in the day. She has her headaches till after lunch.'

'Then you get together for dinner.'

Fleetwood looked sad.

'No. In the afternoon, she has to get ready for the evening. Her hairdresser always takes quite a long time, and her make-up artist, and sometimes her dressmaker. In the evening she goes out. She goes to theatre parties, concert parties, opera parties, ballet parties, art-gallery parties and just plain party parties. All for charity, of course.'

'Couldn't she send the money to the charities and stay at home?' Michael asked.

For a moment, Fleetwood looked puzzled.

'That wouldn't be the same.'

'No, it wouldn't.'

'She says she's *involved*. She's on a lot of committees.' He hesitated and then seemed irritated. 'Anyway, it's none of your business.'

'I'm sorry, I just wondered –'

'Don't.'

Fleetwood pushed his plate aside, though it was still half-full of ice-cream.

'I haven't quite finished,' Michael said when Fleetwood stood up.

'Leave the rest. We're going outside for field and track.'

Behind the house were the extensive sports grounds – a football field, a cricket pitch, an Olympic-sized swimming pool, tennis courts, a half-mile oval running track and, beyond all that, an eighteen-hole golf course.

'Is all of it your father's?' Michael said in awe.

'It's mine,' Fleetwood said. 'He has his own set-up, starting on the other side of my golf course. His sports grounds are so big he gets around them by helicopter – not that he visits them more than once or twice a year, whenever he invites foreign diplomats and generals over for one of his military exhibitions, army manoeuvres or an air display.'

'Are you in a football and cricket team?'

'I don't belong to anything,' Fleetwood retorted haughtily. 'Things belong to me. When I want football or cricket I hire the best professionals and watch them play.'

'That must be great for your school friends,' Michael said.

'I haven't got any. My mother doesn't let me go out to school. She says I'm safer in my own private school at home.'

'And you're the only pupil?'

'Of course. But I have the best teachers and they give me the best marks. If teachers give me anything less than a hundred per cent – out! I have them sacked.'

'Don't you get awfully lonely?' Michael asked.

Fleetwood looked uncomfortable.

'Well, I must admit that sometimes I do get a little lonely. That's why when I saw the commercial for the Young Companions Agency I got in touch with them. At first, my mother said that getting a companion here like that was out of the question.' Fleetwood smiled. 'But I kicked up a rumpus. If I go to her bedroom at about noon, when she's having her first cup of coffee, I can always persuade her to let me do anything I want, as long as I go away and leave her in peace. That's how I got you here. Now, how about the hundred-metre dash? The Agency said you're quite an athlete. Show me!'

'I'm only a little better than average at running,' Michael said modestly. 'But I'm willing to give it a try, if you are.'

'I paid. You run and I'll watch.'

Twenty

Some Fixed Games

Fleetwood stood beside the smooth cinder track, holding a silver starting pistol (loaded with blank cartridges) in one hand and a Swiss stop-watch in the other, to measure the number of seconds Michael would take to run one hundred metres.

'Ready?' Fleetwood demanded.

'I suppose so,' Michael replied, looking up from his crouching position at the start-line. 'I've never run on my own like this before. It seems strange with nobody to race against.'

'You're racing against this watch.'

'Oh, all right.'

Fleetwood pointed the pistol at the sky.

Bang!

Michael ran along the empty track, not quite as fast as he might have run at school. Having crossed the finishing-line, he walked slowly back.

'That wasn't much good,' Fleetwood commented, shaking his head disapprovingly. 'Fourteen-point-nine seconds isn't exactly a world record.'

'It'd be a lot more fun if you ran, too,' Michael

pointed out. 'With a few other kids as well. That'd be a real race.'

Fleetwood looked doubtful.

'I've never tried that,' he said. 'What if I didn't win?'

'It would make you train some more and try harder next time. You'd get better and better, even if you never won. Winning's nicer than losing, everyone knows that, but it doesn't really matter very much if you don't win.'

'All right,' Fleetwood said. 'Enough talk. Let me see some more action. Do it again. And this time you have to beat fourteen seconds.'

Michael shrugged his shoulders and got ready again. Fleetwood set his stop-watch and reloaded the pistol.

Bang!

Michael ran as fast as he could.

When he got back to the start, he was still breathing hard.

'Well?' he said.

'That was a little better. Thirteen-point-eight seconds. A fraction more than a second better.'

'Did you enjoy the difference?' Michael asked, baffled by Fleetwood's attitude.

'No. It was boring.'

'I agree.'

'Do you?' Fleetwood said, smiling, because he was pleased to have someone to agree with. 'We can go inside, if you like. I have some nifty electronic space-travel games.'

'I'd like to see them,' Michael said. He was glad not to be ordered to run by himself a third time.

As they walked side by side back to the house, Fleetwood said: 'If we did run together, would you let me win?'

'What would be the point of having a race if we didn't both really try?'

Fleetwood thought for a moment.

'If we did both really try and I didn't win, would you laugh?'

'Probably!' Michael said, and laughed.

So did Fleetwood, surprising both Michael and himself.

The space-travel games, in Fleetwood's special space-travel games room, proved not to be contests at all. They were only video games fixed so that Fleetwood could never miss and always had perfect scores. When Michael played, the games were fixed so he didn't do very well. He kept looking at the clock on the wall, whose hands seemed to be moving very slowly. Fleetwood noticed Michael's increasing restlessness.

'This isn't much fun either, is it?' Fleetwood said.

'No,' Michael said.

'Michael, there's something I wonder.'

'What?'

'How can I have fun?'

Twenty-one

A Very Unusual School

Michael had almost finished breakfast in Fleetwood's private dining room the next morning by the time Fleetwood came to the table.

'Am I allowed to come to your school?' Michael asked. He missed his friends at his own school.

'"Allowed"? You *have* to come. That's part of your job, to come to my school and make me look good. When we have a quiz, they'll give us difficult questions, and you won't know the answers.'

'How can you be sure you'll know them?'

'The teacher always gives them to me in a written list.'

'Then why have a quiz?'

'To impress Dad. Every time he comes home he gets a report on my quiz scores and grades and general progress and all that.'

'Doesn't he get suspicious when everything is perfect?'

'He, himself, doesn't read the report. He's too busy getting ready for his next business trip. But his secretary looks the report over and tells him it's OK.

If it wasn't OK she'd have to get a lot of explanations from the teachers, so when it's OK everyone's OK.'

'But how can you be sure you're really doing all right?'

'How can I miss?'

'I mean, how do you know you're learning enough?'

'Enough for what?'

'You want to get your GCSEs and A levels and so on, don't you? Don't you hope to go to university one day? Shouldn't you make sure you're keeping up with other kids?'

Fleetwood smiled.

'Of course I'll go to university. Dad can get me into any university in the country.'

Michael decided there would be no point in arguing any more.

'It's getting late. What time are we meant to be in class?'

'Don't panic. There's an Italian cartoon show I usually catch by satellite at about this time. Class can't begin till I get there, so there's no such thing as "late".'

Fleetwood took Michael to the television room to watch a movie about a cat and a mouse in rocket-ships.

'It was better yesterday,' Fleetwood said rather irritably. 'The mouse had a magic lollipop which could make him invisible when he was trapped in a corner. This cartoon's rubbish.'

'Yes, it is,' Michael agreed.

'We may as well go to the classroom. Miss

Allegro's on duty today. She's sometimes good for a laugh, especially when she turns her back to write on the blackboard and I quickly pour glue on her chair.'

'Doesn't she get cross?'

'Of course she does. That's the joke. Anyway, it's more fun than arithmetic.'

'Why doesn't she leave?'

'We pay her plenty. Maybe she will leave soon. They all do. But there are lots more teachers where she came from.'

Michael realised how unhappy Fleetwood was.

After lunch (Michael had a hamburger and a glass of milk; Fleetwood had steamed crocodile nose and papaya juice), sitting on stools at the soda-fountain counter, they talked of this and that. Fleetwood did most of the talking.

'What's it like at a regular school?'

'Well,' Michael said, 'we work and we play. There are all sorts of boys and girls, some clever ones, some not so clever, some who take everything seriously, some who don't, some who are good at singing and making clay pottery, some who are good at football and swimming; all kinds. I have – I used to have – many friends and a couple of enemies. You know.'

'No,' Fleetwood said gloomily. 'I don't.'

He produced a large, red silk handkerchief and loudly blew his nose. Michael realised that the richest boy in Britain was crying. 'I haven't any friends.'

'If you want, I'll be your friend.'

'You will? Honestly? I'll give you anything you say.'

'That isn't the way it works,' Michael said patiently. 'It's no good paying someone to be your friend. He or she has to want to be. All you have to do to get a friend is to be friendly. It's as simple as that.'

'I know what,' Fleetwood said, brightening like sunshine after rain. 'I'll get the Young Companions Agency to rush over another two dozen children. Then we can have real classes and real games, like the ones you used to have at your school. I'll hire some more teachers and some championship sports coaches. We can organise –'

'There's no need to do all that. If your father and mother let you have everything you ask for, why don't you just ask them to let you go to the local school? I'm sure you'd like it.'

'I'll talk to Mum tomorrow before mid-day, when she's only half awake. My chauffeur could take us to school in one of the Rolls-Royces.'

'Let's go on bikes,' Michael said.

'Wow! What a fabulous idea!'

When he told his mother about it the following day, at first she objected.

'There are germs out there,' she said, yawning.

Fleetwood kept persuading her.

'Please, darling,' she groaned. 'Not at this early hour. Mummy has one of her headaches. The Annual Charity Ball for Aged Tennis Players went on till very late. We'll talk some other time.'

Fleetwood loved his mother but it was difficult for him to get at her.

In the evenings, when she was preparing to go out, she was as glamorous as a movie star, with beautiful black hair in curls on top of her head, beautiful black eye-brows and eye-lashes, beautiful pink cheeks and beautiful red lips – and she was too busy for him.

In the mornings, in her bedroom, she seemed to have less hair and her face was pale – and she was too tired for him. He wished she'd stay at home more, get up earlier, and look happy all the time.

'No, Mummy, *please*. Let's talk now. I want to go to a real school like Michael and all the other kids.'

'Who's Michael?' she asked uninterestedly.

'He's my friend. I told you about the Y.C.A.'

'Did you? Oh, yes, of course. All right then. Be careful. Take your credit cards and lots of money. And be sure to get home early. Your Daddy's coming back from Argentina this afternoon, I think. He'll probably be able to give you an appointment from four to four-fifteen.'

'Thanks, Mum,' Fleetwood said. But she had already turned on to her side with her face to the wall and was beginning to snore.

Twenty-two

An Important Lesson

Although the school year was almost over, when the head of the local school heard Fleetwood's famous name on the telephone, she said Fleetwood and Michael could come in straight away. She put them in a class of their own age group to see how they would get on.

'Sometimes children who have had private lessons do quite well. We'll see. Tell Mr and Mrs Pelf you're welcome here and we hope they'll visit us very soon. You may have to do some extra studying during the summer holidays, but I'm sure you'll fit in without difficulty in the autumn.'

Michael was glad to be back in a real classroom, and Fleetwood was delighted, though a bit dazed, by all the bright chatter. He sat in his place at the back of the room quietly until, during history, there was a general discussion on the subject of war.

'War,' one girl said, 'is the silliest thing I ever heard of. It spoils everything.'

Fleetwood spoke up, repeating his father's words:
'Preparing for war makes jobs and prosperity –

and prevents war, usually.'

'What do you know about it?' a boy asked.

'My father happens to be the chairman of Consolidated Universal Associates. That's what I know about it. He's the world's biggest manufacturer of weapons. He employs more people and makes more money than anyone else in Britain.'

'What a waste!' another girl said.

'I'm proud of Consolidated,' Fleetwood said.

'You should be ashamed,' another boy said.

'Now, children,' said the teacher, holding up a hand to silence all of them for a moment. 'We can discuss this important matter calmly and reasonably without starting a war of our own.'

In the playground during the break, Fleetwood said the other children didn't know what they were talking about.

'My dad's the richest man in Britain,' he pointed out.

'Yes, I know,' Michael acknowledged. 'But what's the good of the things he sells? If people use them they destroy each other's cities and everyone in them. And if they don't use the weapons they've spent billions of pounds for nothing. Isn't that true? Isn't it crazy?'

'In a way, I suppose,' Fleetwood said, squirming like a fish caught in a net.

'In every way,' Michael said. 'Why do you think your father has to spend so much time travelling around the world, persuading the leaders of so many countries to buy his weapons? Because they're so expensive and so dangerous that nobody really wants to buy them. Think how much easier it would be for him to sell things they want to buy, things to make life better, like farm machinery, so people could grow enough to eat. Right now, about half the people in the world are starving and they're afraid that one day bombs will blow them to bits.'

Michael paused and thought about bombs.

'If your father sold tractors and ploughs and well-drilling equipment and other things like those, they'd practically sell themselves. Most of the time, he could stay at home.'

'Hmmmm,' Fleetwood murmured thoughtfully.

Twenty-three

Improvements

Fleetwood Pelf Senior was tired, as usual, when he returned home that afternoon. He was a tall, strong man with a smooth, red face, but he was walking with a bent back, his black hair was already turning grey at the sides and there were dark bags under his eyes. He had not had a holiday for years and looked as though he urgently needed one.

He seemed pleased to see his son when they met in the library.

'What's new?' Fleetwood Senior asked, expecting to hear only about new things his son had bought for his own amusement.

Young Fleetwood surprised him by telling him about Michael and their first day together in a real school.

'I've already learnt some good ideas,' said Fleetwood Junior. 'Some of the other kids thought of some and Michael thought of some and I thought of some.'

'That's splendid!' Fleetwood Senior said. He had been afraid that his son would never do anything but play about. 'Tell me all about them.'

The boy was not at all sure that his father would be pleased to hear unfavourable criticism of his big, international trade in weapons and the suggestion that he should switch to farm machines, but young Fleetwood took a deep breath and took the plunge. He talked very seriously for a long time.

Fleetwood Senior happily beamed.

'All that's very interesting,' he said. 'As a matter of fact, I was in London the other day and a group of us were sitting in my club asking ourselves some tough questions about the situation in this country and all over the rest of the world, and by golly! I think you've come up with the answers!'

'Michael helped,' Fleetwood Junior admitted modestly.

'That boy sounds all right,' Fleetwood Senior said. 'I'm looking forward to meeting him.'

'He's my friend,' the boy said. 'I wish he were my brother.'

He repeated everything that Michael had told him, about the deaths of Michael's mother and father, the awful meanness of the Foxes and how they had sent him away from his home to the Young Companions Agency and –

'That organisation will have to be closed down, even though it did help you,' Fleetwood Senior eventually commented. 'Selling children is against the law. But if Michael would like to stay with us I'll adopt him and he'll be part of our family always.'

'Oh, Dad, thank you!'

'Of course, we'll have to ask Michael. He's free to choose whatever he wants to do.'

'But what about the Foxes?' Fleetwood, Junior, asked.

'Don't worry about *them*,' his father said. In the past hour or so, he already seemed to have become about ten years younger – upright, alert, energetic and enthusiastic. What a relief it would be, not having to travel so much, persuading people to waste their money on weapons that were made only to do harm! What a pleasure it would be to make things that only do good! People would be eager to get them! They would come to him! He could stay at home as much as he liked.

'From what you say, I suspect the Foxes could be in serious trouble. I'll get some of my best solicitors working on the case immediately. The Foxes will be out of that house before they know what hit them. We can go on from there.'

'*Thank* you, Dad.'

'Thank *you*, son. And Michael.'

Twenty-four

Hooray for Almost Everyone

When Fleetwood told Michael, over a large strawberry banana split at Fleetwood's soda fountain, that Fleetwood Senior wanted to adopt him, Michael was very pleased that his friend liked him so much.

Michael liked Fleetwood a lot now. They had played some good games with boys and girls from school – roller-skate hockey, bicycle polo and pirates and sailors in the swimming pool. Things had certainly improved since they had met. And no doubt it would be fun and interesting in all sorts of ways to be the foster brother of the richest boy in Britain.

'Do you want Charlie Fox sent to prison?' Fleetwood asked.

Michael remembered all the unhappiness the Foxes had caused, but he shook his head.

'No, thanks all the same. Mr and Mrs Fox and Cuddles will be stuck with each other. They're all so horrible that that'll be enough punishment. There is one thing I do want, though.'

'Name it!' Fleetwood said.

Just then there was a knock at the door and the butler entered the room.

'Fleetwood, a man has arrived who says he has come to collect Michael. Mr Driscoll, he says his name is. Shall I send him away?'

'Yes,' Fleetwood said.

'Oh, no, please, Fleetwood!' Michael protested. 'That's Josh, the person I told you about.'

'Ask him to come in,' Fleetwood told the butler.

The reunion of Josh and Michael was a happy one. Michael introduced him to Fleetwood.

'Fleetwood's my best friend,' Michael said. 'We're going to be brothers. His father's going to adopt me.'

Josh looked surprised, and pleased.

'Anna and I were very worried about you when we saw you in the Fizzo commercial. I've had quite a time tracking you down. The police gave me the Foxes' address. That Fox character didn't want to give me any information about you, but I convinced him he'd better. Mr Poindexter was a little difficult at first, but I managed to make him talk sense. I thought I'd have some real trouble here, coming to rescue you. But you're all right, are you? Are you sure?'

'I'm fine, Josh. But it was great of you to look for me.'

'Anna will be pleased,' Josh said. 'We were going to invite you to live with us in the caravan, but it would have been a bit of a squeeze. She's expecting a baby in the autumn.'

Fleetwood and Michael took Josh to meet

Fleetwood's father. When he had heard the story of Josh's search, he said, 'You deserve a medal!'

Michael had a better idea.

'I said there's one thing I want,' he told Fleetwood Senior. 'When the Foxes are put out of my house –'

'They'll be out by tomorrow,' Fleetwood Senior promised.

'Well, I want Josh and Anna to have my house,' Michael said. 'There'll be plenty of room for them and their baby, and there's a nice garden.'

'That would be wonderful,' Josh said.

When Fleetwood Senior heard that Josh made his living by driving trucks while his wife was a waitress, he said he'd let Josh have enough money to start a restaurant of their own. Josh was almost overwhelmed. He said he didn't know how long it would take but he'd pay back every penny, and Fleetwood Senior said there wasn't any hurry.

'You'll be able to stop going on all those long trips,' he said. 'I know how bad they can be.'

After a big lunch (steak etc.), Josh headed for home, to tell Anna all the good news.

The next morning, Fleetwood Junior told Michael some more good news.

'Things are looking up! Mum says that now Dad's going to be at home most of the time she isn't going to any more of those charity parties. She's going to send the money straight to the charities, as you suggested. But she has plans for a party at home – for all the kids in our class. She says if it hadn't been for you and them none of this would have happened. We'll have a party in a huge tent, like a circus tent, beside the playing fields, and we'll all dress up as clowns.'

'That'll be great!' Michael said.

'And that reminds me,' Fleetwood said with a grin. 'Speaking of the playing fields, I challenge you to a hundred-metre race.'

'You're on,' said Michael, and they went out together, arm in arm.